This book just ate my dog!

Richard BYRNE

WALKIES!

OXFORD

UNIVERSITY PRESS

Bella was taking her dog for a stroll across the page when . . .

. . . something very odd happened.

Bella's dog disappeared.

'Hello Bella.
What's up?'
said Ben.

**Ben decided
to investigate.**

But Ben disappeared too.

Help zoomed into sight . . .

. . . then vanished.

Things were getting ridiculous.

'I'll just have to sort this out myself,' thought Bella.

But . . .

Sometime later
a note appeared.

It read . . .

Dear reader,

It would be lovely if you
could kindly HELP US!
Please turn this book
on its side and SHAKE...

Bella
x

1. Turn book around

2. Shake

...and SHAKE and SHAKE and SHAKE!

...and one last little wiggle. Thank you. Bella x

Everybody reappeared . . .

. . . and things got back to normal.

Well, almost!

Dear reader,
Please tell this book to promise
not to be so naughty next time
you read it.
Thank you.
Bella
x